OTHER PICTURE BOOKS
BY MITSUMASA ANNO

Anno's Alphabet
Anno's Animals
Anno's Britain
Anno's Counting Book
Anno's Counting House
Anno's Italy
Anno's Journey
Anno's Magical ABC
Anno's Medieval World
Anno's Mysterious Multiplying Jar
Anno's USA
The King's Flower
The Unique World of Mitsumasa Anno

British Library Cataloguing
in Publication Data
Anno, Mitsumasa
Anno's flea market
I. Title
895.6'35 [J] PZ7
ISBN 0-370-30591-4

Copyright © Kuso-Kobo 1983
Printed and bound in Japan for
The Bodley Head Ltd,
9 Bow Street, London WC2E 7AL
English publication rights arranged through
Kurita-Bando Literary Agency with Dowaya
First published in Great Britain 1984

ANNO'S FLEA MARKET

Mitsumasa Anno

/681

THE BODLEY HEAD

LONDON   SYDNEY

TORONTO

Early on a Sunday morning in the market square of an old walled town things begin to stir. A farmer arrives with his cart piled high with produce, a dealer in old cars pulls them into place, a flower seller puts up his stall. The market – the flea market – is coming to life.

No one seems to know exactly why it is called a flea market; certainly there are no fleas for sale. Some people say it is because you can buy anything there 'from an elephant to a flea'. Others say that you used to be able to see sideshows of performing fleas in open-air markets, others that you ran the risk of catching fleas because everything was so dirty. Whatever the reason, a flea market is what it is called, and in this one you can find almost everything you can think of, from hair restorer to candy-floss, from bagpipes to warming-pans. And most of the things on display are not new or even in working order; there is a lot of what appears to be just junk, used electric light bulbs, spectacles with only one lens, clocks with broken springs, ancient tools, old clothes. But what everything in the flea market has in common is that it once belonged to someone, was made by them or used by them. It might even have belonged to your mother, to your grandfather or your great-great-grandparents. Every single object in the market has a story behind it.

Some of the things will puzzle you, others will make you laugh. Some will tell you about the world as it used to be, others of the world as it is today. And there are certainly plenty of surprises to be found if you look hard enough!

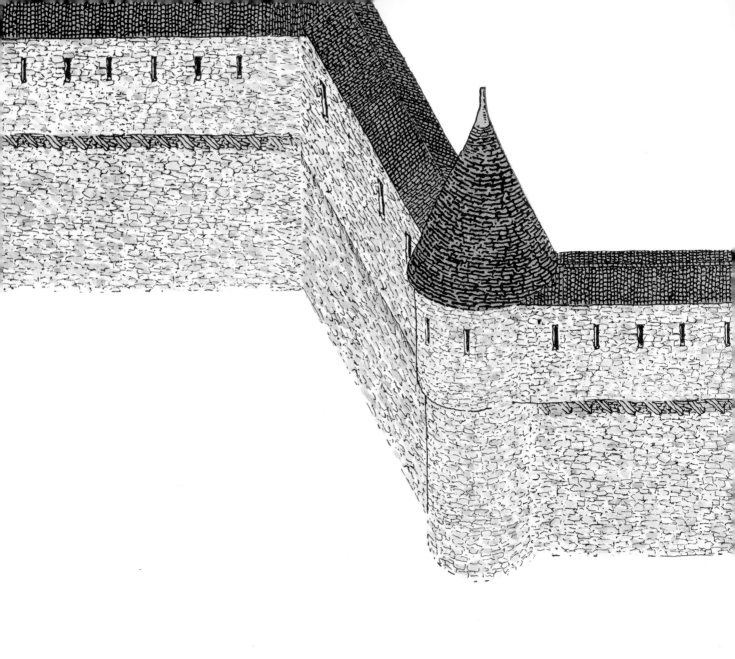

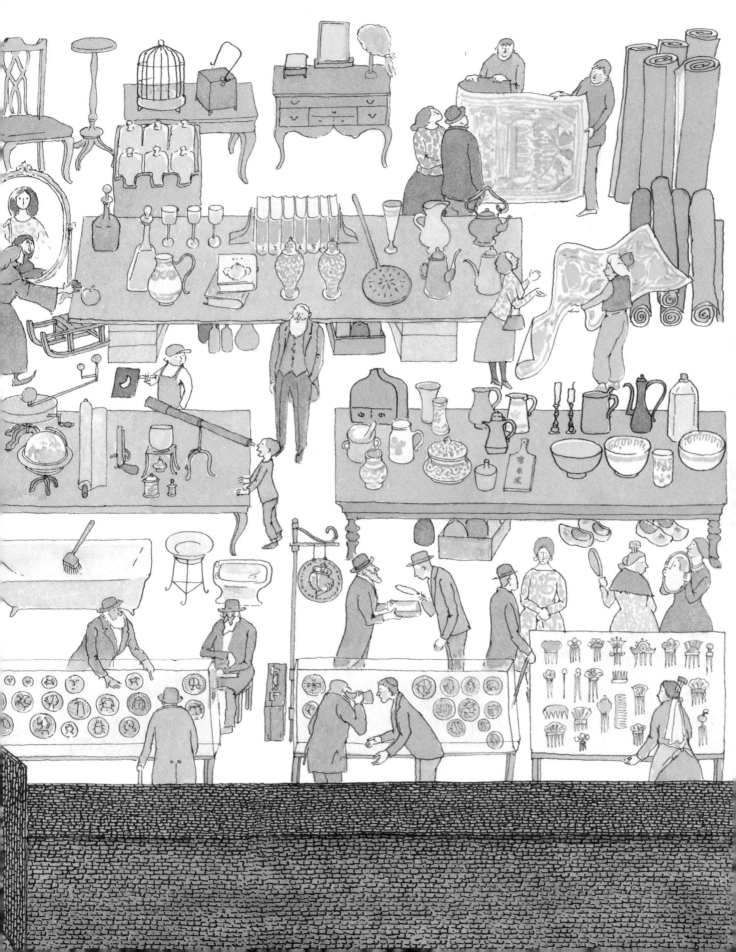

I would like to tell you a story about a bowl, a bowl that you could probably only find today in a flea market. It is a hard wooden bowl of great width and depth, hollowed out from the trunk of a huge tree. I am told that it was once used for kneading dough in the making of bread. When I first saw the bowl and heard its story I started to wonder about the woman who had made bread in it, about the man who had carved it and about the woodcutter who had brought the wood in from the forest. I even wondered about the tree itself. After all this wondering, what else could I do but buy the bowl? I wish you could see it; it is one of my most precious possessions.

I believe that each one of us is born with the skill to distinguish handmade objects from those that are made by machine, and that we are also born with the ability to tell old from new. It goes against these instincts in all of us to make mass-produced objects look like handmade ones or, perhaps worse still, to make brand new things look old. Everything belongs to its own time and should age accordingly.

Take this book, for instance. It was published in 1984 and for that year remains a new book, but then it starts to age. Make a note of the date you first looked at it and then make a list of the things you have noticed in it. I would then be very happy if you would come back to it after a period of time, make a new list of what you see and then compare the two lists. I think you will be surprised at the difference in them. This book will not then be a new one – and, who knows, it may well be found in a flea market one day.

Mitsumasa Anno

Mitsumasa Anno was born in Tsuwano, a small historic town in the
western part of Japan, in 1926, and he has long been acknowledged as one of
Japan's leading illustrators and book designers. He graduated from
Yamaguchi Teacher Training College and worked as a primary school teacher
for several years before starting his career as an artist. While teaching young
children he came to the firm belief that the worlds created by pictures and
by words are different, and in *Anno's Flea Market* he provides us with an
absorbing and purely pictorial world that demonstrates also his concern for
history in its simplest but most far-reaching sense. Every one of the things he
shows us has a unique story of its own to tell, and in this book the artist gives
us the opportunity to explore 'story' and 'history' together.

Mitsumasa Anno has travelled widely in Europe and North America, as
this fascinating and diverse collection of objects testifies, and now lives in
Tokyo with his wife, daughter, and son Masaichiro, who has collaborated
with his father on three previous picture books.